W9-DGH-751

An I Can Read Book™

Rafi and Rosi CARNIVAL!

Lulu Delacre

rayo

HarperCollins*Publishers*

Para Matthew,
mi sobrinito

HarperCollins®, ☂®, and I Can Read Book® are trademarks of HarperCollins Publishers Inc.
Rayo is an imprint of HarperCollins Publishers Inc.

Library of Congress Cataloging-in-Publication Data
Delacre, Lulu.
  Rafi and Rosi : Carnival! / Lulu Delacre.— 1st ed.
    p.   cm. — (An I can read book)
  Summary: Two Latin American tree frogs, mischievous Rafi and his younger sister Rosi, enjoy the events of Puerto Rico's Carnival season.
  ISBN-10: 0-06-073597-X — ISBN-10: 0-06-073598-8 (lib. bdg.)
  ISBN-13: 978-0-06-073597-5 — ISBN-13: 978-0-06-073598-2 (lib. bdg.)
  [1. Tree frogs—Fiction.   2. Frogs—Fiction.   3. Brothers and sisters—Fiction.   4. Carnival—Puerto Rico—Fiction.
5. Puerto Rico—Fiction.]   I. Title: Carnival!   II. Title.   III. Series.
PZ7.D383165Raf 2006   2005002675
[E]—dc22   CIP
                                                                                                                                    AC

1 2 3 4 5 6 7 8 9 10 ❖ First Edition

Contents

Glossary	4
Queen for a Day	5
X-ray Eyes	25
Terrible Mask	43
Did You Know . . .	61

Glossary

Ahorita (**ah-oh-REE-tah**): A Puerto Rican way of saying "later."

¡Ay, no! (**EYE-NOH**): Oh, no!

Bueno (**BWEH-noh**): Well (as an interjection); good.

Coquí (**coh-KEE**): A tiny tree frog found in Puerto Rico that is named after its song.

Doña (**DOH-nyah**): Title of courtesy and respect preceding a woman's first name.

Hola (**OH-lah**): Hello.

¡Perfecto! (**pehr-FEHC-toh**): Perfect!

Periscope: An optical instrument used for viewing objects that are out of one's field of vision.

Ponce: Southern city of Puerto Rico.

Reina (**RAY-nah**): Queen.

Rey Momo (**ray MOH-moh**): King Momo. The king of the Carnival of Ponce.

Sardine: Small fish; age-old character with Spanish roots that is part of the Carnival of Ponce.

Seguro (**Seh-GUH-roh**): Of course; sure.

Sí (**SEE**): Yes.

Tía (**TEE-ah**): Aunt.

Vejigante (**veh-hee-GAN-tay**): Masquerader from Puerto Rico named after the handmade noisemakers, or *vejigas*, that he or she carries.

Queen
for a Day

Rafi Coquí was busy

making a mask

for the Carnival in Ponce.

"Rafi, come out!"

Rosi called from outside.

"Push me on the swing!"

6

"Ahorita," said Rafi. "Later."

"PLEASE," Rosi begged.

Rafi didn't want to stop

making his mask.

He looked around for something

his little sister could do.

Next to him lay the Carnival issue

of the newspaper.

It gave him an idea.

"Hey, go find

a queen outfit!"

he said.

"A queen outfit?" asked Rosi.

"You could be the queen
of this year's parade," said Rafi.

"I'm sure you would win."

"You really think so?"
asked Rosi.

"*Seguro,*" Rafi said. "Sure.
Doña Carmen, next door,
is one of the judges."

Rosi came in

and picked up the newspaper.

She looked at the pictures

for a long time.

"Hmm . . . ," she said.

Her eyes sparkled.

She ran to the dress-up chest.

She lifted out

the pale green scarf,

the hot pink scarf,

the sky blue scarf,

and the crown with red feathers.

10

She tried them on.
She skipped and twirled
in front of the mirror.

"Hmm . . . ," she said.
"Something is missing."

11

Rosi tiptoed into her mother's room
and put on a string of fake pearls,
two silvery bracelets,
and big rings
on each and every finger.
She danced and curtsied
to the imaginary crowd
in the mirror.

"Hmm . . . ," she said.
"Something
is still missing."

Rosi slid her fingers
into her mother's
makeup drawer
and found
a very pink lipstick.
She painted her lips
shiny and sweet.

"I'm going to be the Carnival Queen!"
Rosi said.

She marched out the front door

and slammed it behind her.

Rafi looked up.

Had his sister just left?

"Rosi!" he called.

Rosi skipped all the way

to Doña Carmen's house.

Rafi followed her.

Rosi opened the gate.

"*Hola*, Rosi," Doña Carmen greeted her.

"Are you ready for Carnival?"

"*Hola*, Doña Carmen," said Rosi.

"I am here to be chosen as the queen."

"Oh, Rosi," said Doña Carmen.

"I am sorry, but in this contest

you have to be older."

"But Rafi told me I was sure to win,"
Rosi said, her mouth now
half its usual size.
Rafi came up to the gate.
Doña Carmen stared at him.
Rafi shrugged.

"Let's go home, Rosi," Rafi said.

"I'll push you on the swing."

"NO!" Rosi yelled.

She ran all the way back home

and deep into her room.

Standing outside Rosi's room,

Rafi heard her sob.

What could he do now?

He went out to the backyard.

In the corner he saw

his old wagon.

"I know!" he said.

Rafi ran back inside.
When he came out again,
he had a big box
filled with things.

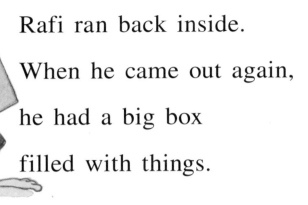

In it, he had
empty tin cans,
string,
paper streamers and glue,
scissors,
and all his paints and brushes.

He set to work.

He cut and pasted,

glued and tied,

painted and fixed.

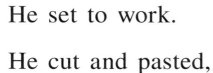

When he was finally done,

he stood up and looked

at what he had made.

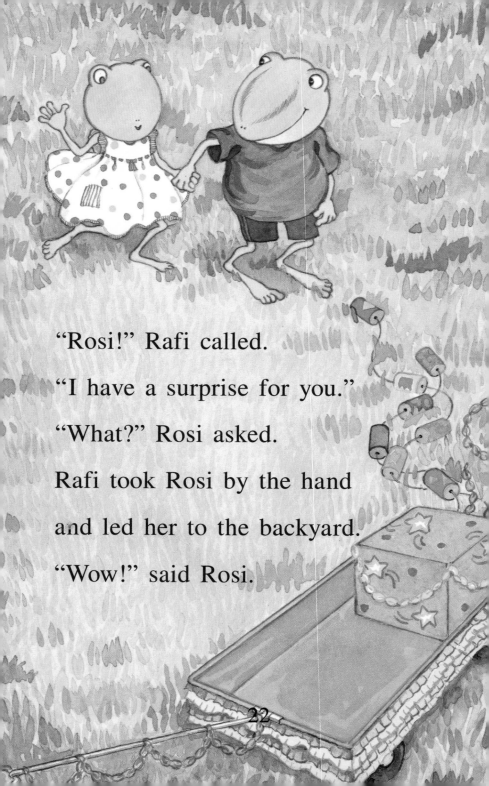

"Rosi!" Rafi called.

"I have a surprise for you."

"What?" Rosi asked.

Rafi took Rosi by the hand

and led her to the backyard.

"Wow!" said Rosi.

"With this float," Rafi said,

"you'll be queen for a day."

Rosi gave Rafi a big hug.

That afternoon,

on the wagon-turned-float,

Rosi beamed

as she went up and down their street

in her very own parade.

"*¡Perfecto!*" Rafi said.

"With this second mirror

in my periscope,

I'll be able to look

all the way down the street

without going out."

"Rafi, the parade!" Rosi called.

Rafi hid his periscope.

"Today Carnival starts," said Rosi.

"Tía Marta says the parade

will go by very soon.

We need to go out front to see it!"

"Oh, yes, the parade," said Rafi.

"I'll watch it from here."

He sat down next to the closed window
and leaned his head back.

"You have to come out," said Rosi.

"You can't see the parade from there."

"Oh, yes I can," said Rafi.

"I have x-ray eyes."

"X-ray eyes?" asked Rosi.

"Yes," said Rafi. "I'll show you.

Just stand by the door

so you can hear me call out

who's coming up the street."

"Can you really see
through walls?"
asked Rosi.
"Of course," said Rafi.
"I told you,
I have x-ray eyes."

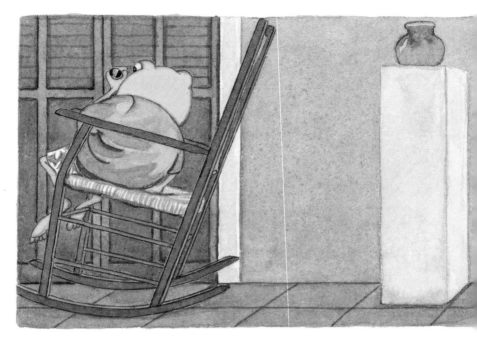

Rosi went outside.

The sidewalks were crowded.

And the music from many drums

got louder and louder.

From inside the house Rafi shouted,

"Here comes Rey Momo

in a red and yellow outfit!"

Rosi jumped up and down

to get a better look.

Rafi was right about the king.

Rosi looked at the tall windows

that opened onto the balcony.

The shutters were closed.

"Rafi must be guessing," she said.

"Look, Rosi!" Rafi called.

"The float with the Carnival Queen."

Rosi stretched

to look around the potted palm.

32

"The queen is wearing sequins
and peacock feathers," Rafi added.
The young queen waved to Rosi.
And she was dressed
just like Rafi said she was.

"Wow!" Rosi cried out to Rafi.
"How did you do that?"
But Rafi didn't hear her.
He was busy saying
who was coming next.

"Rosi!" Rafi yelled.
"Here come the *vejigantes*
with their scary masks!"
"There's something strange,"
Rosi mumbled.

Rosi tiptoed into the house.

Rafi was still on the rocker.

He was bent over a cardboard tube.

Rosi went back outside.

Then she noticed

that the tube stuck out

through a missing slat in the shutters.

Rosi looked

right into the tube.

"*¡Ay, no!*" Rafi said.

The tube disappeared into the window.

"Aha!" Rosi said, nodding her head.

Rosi raced inside.

"What was that

you were holding?" she asked.

Rafi looked down.

Then he looked into Rosi's eyes.

"Bueno . . . ," he said.

Finally, he took out his periscope.

"With this," he said, "you can look
all the way down the street
without ever leaving the room."
"How?" Rosi asked.
Rafi told Rosi how one slanted mirror
reflected the image of the street
onto another slanted mirror
closer to you.

Rosi tried it. It really worked.

"But Rafi," Rosi said,

giving back the periscope,

"I like to see the floats up close."

"Hmm . . . ," Rafi said.

"I guess outside you feel

like part of the Carnival. . . ."

"*¡Sí, sí!*" yelled Rosi.

"Let's go,

before it's all over!"

They ran out the door.

Perched on the balcony
of Tía Marta's house,
Rafi and Rosi Coquí
waved, giggled,
and chanted.

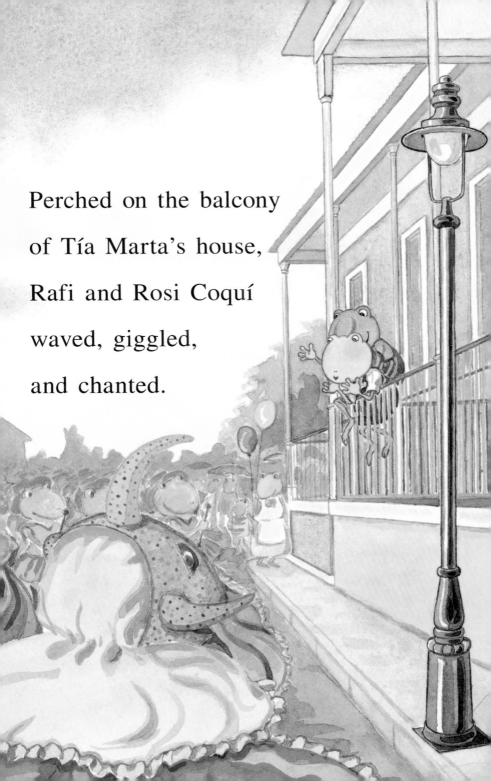

They were thrilled
by the sounds and sights
of the first day
of Carnival.

The crowd was excited.

Young and old

lined the path of the parade

during the last hours of Carnival.

"Climb up the tree," said Rafi,

"so you can see

the Sardine's funeral.

Rey Momo leads it."

"A funeral?" asked Rosi.

"Is that why everybody is crying?"

"It's a show," said Rafi.

"You pretend to be sad

that the sardine fish has died."

"Yes," said Rosi,

"I see the queen giggling."

"They say," Rafi added,

"that the Sardine's coffin

is full of candy.

I hope I get a lot. Don't you?"

46

But Rosi didn't answer.

She was so charmed

by the singing and moaning

now on the stage.

Rafi looked at Rosi.

"This is it," he said to himself.

47

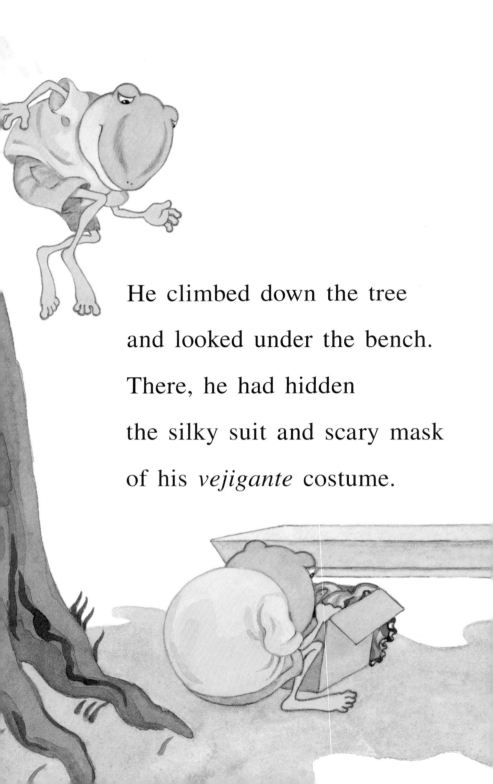

He climbed down the tree
and looked under the bench.
There, he had hidden
the silky suit and scary mask
of his *vejigante* costume.

For Rafi,

the best part of being a *vejigante*

was running around

scaring your friends.

"I bet Rosi will scream."

Rafi grinned.

"This year's mask

is my scariest."

Hidden behind his mask,
Rafi blended into the crowd
and walked through it.
He picked a good spot.
Then, at just the right moment,
he jumped in front of Rosi
and screamed, "ARRRGH!"
"*¡Ay no!*" Rosi yelped.
"Go away!"

Rosi climbed down the tree
and darted across the plaza.
She slid under the stage
to hide from the *vejigante*
and its terrible mask.
She could barely breathe.

Slowly, Rosi calmed down,

and she peeked from behind

the stage's paper lining.

She wanted to find Rafi

so she could tell him

what had happened.

But the terrible mask

popped up wherever she looked.

She watched the *vejigante* get closer.

The closer he got to Rosi,

the faster her heart beat.

"Where is Rafi?" she wondered.

The mean *vejigante*
took off his terrible mask,
and Rosi let out
the smallest cry. . . .

It was Rafi!

"How dare he!" she said.

"He knows how scared I am
of *vejigantes*."

"Rosi!" Rafi called.

"Where are you?

Look, it's just me. ROSI!"

But Rosi kept silent.

Rosi saw Rafi
talk to vendors.

She saw him go back and look
where they had been sitting.

She watched him drop his mask
to climb the tallest tree
and search the crowd.
But Rosi didn't come out.

Then Rafi came

to the edge of the stage.

"I've lost my little sister!"

Rosi heard him moan.

And something

melted deep inside her.

She smiled a little smile.

"I'm here!" Rosi yelled,
leaping out of her hiding place.
"Rosi!" Rafi sighed.

He ran to Rosi

and lifted her in the air.

At that moment

a sweet shower fell.

59

Candy pieces

rained that night,

from the Queen

of Carnival,

for everyone to share.

Did You Know . . .

. . . About Carnival?

Every year around February, Carnival brings merriment to the streets. In Spain and many Latin American countries, people celebrate with music, parades, and food and drink for a week before Ash Wednesday.

Carnival in Ponce, Puerto Rico, started in 1858. Today, the tradition-loving people of this southern city celebrate with age-old characters, many of whom have roots in Spain. The Momo King, the *vejigantes*, and the Sardine are among these characters. You have to be selected to be the King or Queen of Carnival. However, anyone can be a *vejigante* and roam around scaring others with papier-mâché masks, clownlike costumes, and the *vejigas*, or noisemakers, after which these characters are named.

For seven days, young and old celebrate with a pageant of queens, floats, bands, and baton twirlers. The Sardine's funeral closes the week with the Carnival Queen taking fistfuls of candy from the coffin to shower on the children below.

. . . How to Make a Wagon Float?

You will need: a wagon, paper streamers in two contrasting colors, tape and glue, cardboard box (optional), 8 to 10 empty cans, a roll of string, construction paper, scissors

1) Fringe the streamers. Starting from the bottom of the wagon, tape the streamers in layers to the sides, alternating colors. All sides should be completely covered.

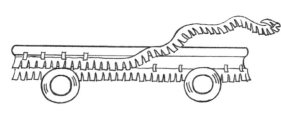

2) You can decorate a cardboard box to place in the wagon as a throne.

3) Wash each can. Have an adult remove the top lids of the cans and make a small hole in the bottom of each can. Cover the cans with construction paper in bright colors. You can draw designs on the papers if you wish.

4) Take a long piece of string and thread it through the hole in a can. Make a big knot on the inside. Thread the string through another can, knot it, and continue until you have four or five cans secured. Repeat the process with additional string and cans.

5) Secure the strings of cans to the back of the wagon by taping the strings to its underside.

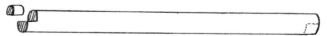

When you pull the wagon, the cans will make noise, announcing your arrival!

. . . How to Make a Periscope?

You will need: a cardboard tube from a wrapping paper roll, two small oval mirrors that fit inside the tube, scissors, black duct tape

1) Cut the top one-third from one end of the tube and the bottom one-third of the other end, about 1 inch from the edge.

2) Tape the mirrors parallel to each other on opposite sides of the tube openings, covering the openings with the tape, as shown.

mirror — cover hole with black tape

cover with black tape

mirror

3) Clean the mirrors. In the mirror closest to you, you will see the image that the other mirror reflects. Look carefully because the image will be small.

4) Now, try to look inside a room without being seen!

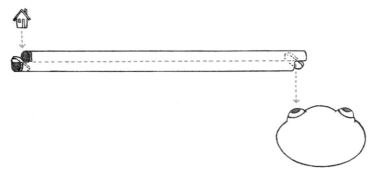

. . . How to Make a *Vejigante* Mask?

Vejigante masks are made out of papier-mâché. Traditional molds are made of clay or cement. Real cow horns are used as molds for the mask's horns. Here is a simpler version.

You will need: a round, blown-up balloon as big as your head, scissors, newspaper strips, water, all-purpose flour, plastic bowl, construction paper circles cut 8 to 10 inches in diameter, tape, acrylic paints in bright colors, brushes, wide elastic band

1) Have an adult help you cook one part flour to two parts water until the mixture turns into a watery paste. Let the paste cool.

2) Hold the balloon on top of a work surface. Wet the paper strips in the paste mixture and gently smooth them onto one side of the balloon. Repeat until you have covered half of the balloon in at least three layers of paper. Place the balloon on its uncovered side in a plastic bowl to let dry at least overnight.

3) Take a circle of construction paper at least 8 inches in diameter.

Cut in half. Roll together to make a slender cone and tape along the edge. Make half-inch cuts along the bottom of each cone. These cones will be your mask's horns. Make several.

4) When your mask is dry, pop the balloon and remove it. Try the mask on, and then cut the edges of the mask to fit your face.

5) Draw openings for the eyes and mouth and cut them out.

6) Flatten the frayed cone edges against the mask and tape the horns onto the top and/or sides of the mask.

7) Use more flour paste and strips of newspaper to cover the horns, smoothing the paper and applying enough strips to securely attach the horns to the mask. Then cover all edges of the mask, including the edges of the eyes and mouth, with small paper strips wet in flour paste. Let dry overnight.

8) Paint your dry mask in bright colors with acrylic paint. Traditional masks from Ponce are often decorated with dots of many colors. Let dry.

9) Have an adult help you attach a wide elastic band to the back of the mask so you can wear it.

Masquerade!